# AN ACTOR

**Jatin Sharma**

The confectionery shop was calm, with only a couple of customers browsing through the shelves.Ramesh leaned back in his chair behind the counter , the faint buzz of a fan doing little to dispel the sticky air. His square face, pale and sharp-jawed, was bathed in the cool glow of his phone as he watched a grainy, violent scene unfold—some cheap thriller about a serial killer.

Around him, the shop bustled faintly. Sumit ji, their old servant, shuffled between shelves, his hands deftly picking out items for the occasional customer. The clatter of goods being rearranged punctuated the muffled hum of the store. A customer approached the counter, placing a modest pile of household items down before pulling out his phone.

"How much?" the man asked, polite but firm.

Ramesh didn't look up, his eyes glued to the bloody climax unfolding on his screen. With an almost lazy wave of his hand, he said, "Wait just a minute, sir."

Seconds later, he finally put his phone down and squinted at the calculator, punching in numbers. "That'll be 550."

The man tapped away on his phone, completing the payment. "Thank you, sir," he said, his tone tinged with the weariness of the day. Ramesh offered a brief nod before slumping back into his chair, earbuds finding their way back into his ears. From behind the counter, only the crown of his head was visible, bobbing faintly to the distant echo of gunshots and snarling dialogue.

The glass door swung open without ceremony as Ramesh's father entered, a burlap bag slung over one shoulder. His movements were quiet, deliberate, the kind born of years spent navigating the narrow aisles of the streets . He set the bag against the wall and approached his son with measured steps, standing silently behind him.

Ramesh remained oblivious, engrossed in the chaos playing out on his screen.

"Is this the climax?" the father asked suddenly, his voice slicing through the bubble of sound around Ramesh.

Startled, Ramesh jerked upright, the blood draining from his face. "Oh! I didn't see you coming," he stammered, pulling out his earbuds and flashing an awkward grin.

His father patted him on the shoulder and eased into the adjacent chair. "No problem, son. Neither would a burglar see you, sitting here like that."

Ramesh chuckled nervously. "That's why we have cameras."

The older man scoffed. "Cameras have their purpose, but I doubt your one in our home ."

He pulled a notebook from beneath the counter and began jotting something down. Ramesh stretched, sighing deeply, his frustration barely masked. "Can I go back to my movie now?"

His father raised his eyebrows, feigning shock. "Can I say no?"

Ramesh shot him a knowing look. "Then you'll lose another half-hour."

The father shook his head, letting the remark hang in the warm, heavy air. "Stay till eight," he said finally.

"I've got a match at five," Ramesh replied, already re-inserting his earbuds.

His father frowned but didn't push the matter, instead calling out for Sumit ji.

he evening in Andheri was full of chaos—vendors shouting prices, children darting between carts, and the relentless honking of impatient motorists. The streets pulsed with life, an endless rhythm of human energy and clamor that seemed to define the area . Ramesh maneuvered his bike through the throng, the engine sputtering slightly before catching rhythm. His brow furrowed as he weaved past hawkers and pedestrians, the heat of the day lingering in the air despite the setting sun.

Bright lights from roadside stalls glinted off his visor, casting fragmented reflections that danced in his peripheral vision. The smell of fried snacks mingled with the metallic tang of the city's exhaust. Somewhere, a radio played an old Bollywood tune, its melody lost in the cacophony. Yet amidst the chaos, Ramesh moved with a practiced ease, his movements calculated and precise. His fingers tightened around the handlebars as he navigated a particularly crowded junction, the din of honking horns rising to a fever pitch.

As the noise of the street began to fade, he entered a quieter neighbourhood. The transformation was stark; the bustling chaos of Andheri gave way to a serene locality lined with modest, well-kept houses. The streets here were wider, the air cooler, and the atmosphere more subdued. Ramesh pulled up in front of one such house, its facade painted a warm cream color that glowed softly under the streetlights. The front yard was tidy, with a small garden of marigolds and hibiscus adding splashes of color to the scene.

He parked his bike and approached the door, his footsteps echoing faintly on the tiled pathway. His knuckles tapped a familiar rhythm against the wood, the sound crisp in the stillness of the evening. After a moment, the door creaked open, revealing a middle-aged woman with kind, welcoming eyes. She wore a simple cotton saree, her demeanor exuding warmth.

"Ramesh, how are you, son?" she asked, her voice tinged with genuine affection.

"All good, aunty. Where's Amit?" he replied, his tone easy and familiar.

The woman turned slightly, her voice rising to a shrill call. "Amit! Ramesh is here!"

Amit appeared moments later, his face breaking into a wide grin. His casual attire and relaxed demeanor contrasted with the charged energy of the street outside. "Let's go," he said, clasping Ramesh's hand in a quick, friendly gesture. Together, they stepped back into the evening, the door closing softly behind them, shutting out the cozy warmth of the house.

The two friends mounted the motorbike, Amit settling into the backseat. Ramesh started the engine, the machine's low hum blending seamlessly with the distant murmur of the city. They rode through the streets, the wind rushing past as they left the residential area behind. The road ahead stretched wide, leading them toward the open expanse of the local ground where their destination awaited.

Amit sat with a thoughtful expression, leaning slightly forward as he spoke. "Surjeet will be there," he said, his voice carrying a mix of curiosity and excitement. "He came back from Europe last week. Heard he bought a new sedan after that big deal his company struck in Dubai. Gotta say, he's living the dream now."

Ramesh tightened his grip on the handlebars, his voice low and rough. "Good for him. Really, good."

The comment hung in the air, heavy with unspoken meaning. Without another word, Ramesh twisted the throttle, the bike accelerating smoothly. The landscape blurred, city lights giving way to the shadowy outlines of trees and quieter roads. The hum of the engine seemed to grow louder in the absence of conversation.

After a stretch of silence, Ramesh spoke abruptly. "Will Tony be coming today?" His tone carried a sharp edge, as if the question was charged with more than casual interest.

Amit hesitated before answering, his voice cautious. "Yeah, he said he would. But you know, everyone's keeping their distance from him these days. His dad... and, well, that incident. He was part of it too."

Ramesh's jaw tightened visibly, and when he spoke, his words were laced with bitterness. "Hypocrites. They're just scared of facing someone who doesn't bother hiding his real self."

Amit tilted his head slightly, puzzled. "The what?"

Ramesh didn't glance back, his focus fixed on the road ahead. "I mean, we're all guilty in some way. Everyone's a criminal in their own right. The difference is, some don't bother pretending otherwise."

Amit shifted in his seat, his expression uncertain. He glanced around as if measuring the distance to their destination, his unease palpable. "How much further?" he asked, his tone betraying his impatience.

Ramesh raised his head slightly, his eyes glinting with a sharp intensity as he shifted gears. The engine roared in response, the sound cutting through the stillness of the night.

The road stretched on, its surface illuminated by the twin beams of the bike's headlights. The city seemed to recede further into the background, its noise and chaos replaced by a quieter, more introspective atmosphere. The two friends rode in silence, their thoughts as tumultuous as the journey itself, the destination looming ever closer.

Night fell softly over the football arena, its floodlights cutting through the darkness and casting long, stark shadows across the turf. The crisp scent of freshly cut grass hung in the cool air, mingling with the faint aroma of sweat and adrenaline. The steady thud of a ball echoed rhythmically, mingling with bursts of laughter and shouts from the players. Beyond the net, a group of boys played with unrelenting energy, their voices cutting through the night as they sprinted, dodged, and weaved in a flurry of motion.

"Pass it here!" one of them yelled, his voice sharp and urgent, his outstretched arm slicing through the glow of the lights. Another countered, already sprinting ahead, "I'm open!" The game was a frenzy of motion—feet pounding against the turf, bodies colliding, the ball a shared heartbeat as it darted back and forth between players. The crowd on the sidelines clapped and cheered, their excitement rising with every near miss and successful goal.

Meanwhile, in a nearby alley, the atmosphere was quieter yet still alive with the echoes of the match. Ramesh and Amit walked side by side, their pace unhurried yet purposeful. The soft shuffle of their shoes against the pavement seemed to underscore the distant roar of the game. The smell of damp concrete mingled with the faint rustle of leaves and the occasional buzz of a streetlamp struggling to stay lit.

Ahead of them, under a flickering streetlight, a weathered bench served as a throne for Surjeet and his group of friends. The air around them was hazy with cigarette smoke, curling in languid spirals before disappearing into the night. They lounged with an air of practiced indifference, their laughter punctuating the stillness like sharp bursts of static. Surjeet's face lit up as he spotted Ramesh and Amit approaching, his grin wide and welcoming.

"Man, you've gotten slender since the last time I saw you," Surjeet called out, rising from the bench and extending a hand to Ramesh. His tone was playful, but his sharp eyes missed nothing.

Ramesh matched his grin, clasping Surjeet's hand in a firm shake before leaning in to bump shoulders. "Well, you know, I started playing more since you left," he said, his voice light but tinged with something deeper.

Surjeet's smirk deepened, his tone turning teasing. "Makes sense, but don't you think it's time you started playing a different game—like money-making?"

Ramesh's grin froze for just a second too long. He clenched his fists subtly, the movement almost imperceptible as he shifted his weight. His gaze slipped away from Surjeet's probing eyes, the tension between them hanging in the air like an unspoken truth. But Ramesh's voice remained steady, even casual, as he replied.

"Well, I heard you bought a new car," he said, steering the conversation to safer ground.

"Yeah, brother," Surjeet replied, his grin broadening as he leaned back. "You should come over sometime. We'll go for a ride, just like the old days on that rusty scooter of mine."

"Sure, sure. I'd love that," Ramesh said quickly, nodding with a forced enthusiasm.

Before the moment could stretch further, a voice interrupted from the bench. "Hey, are we all set? These guys from Bangalore are supposed to be really good. We're playing short passes, right?"

"Right," Ramesh replied, his tone firm, the words almost a command.

"Right," Surjeet echoed, his eyes still lingering on Ramesh with a trace of curiosity that went unspoken.

Ramesh turned toward him, his expression carefully neutral but his words pointed. "By the way, where's Tony?"

Surjeet scoffed, the sharpness of his tone cutting through the night. "You mean that drug dealer?"

"He's still our friend," Ramesh said flatly, his voice unwavering as his gaze met Surjeet's.

Surjeet raised an eyebrow, his skepticism evident. "Our?"

A beat of silence passed between them, heavy and unresolved. Finally, Ramesh shrugged, brushing off the question like dust from his shoulder. "I'll play center," he said, his tone signaling the end of the conversation.

Surjeet rolled his eyes, the tension dissipating as the group began gathering their things. Their chatter grew louder as they moved toward the glowing turf, the anticipation of the match pulling them forward.

The arena buzzed with energy as the teams stepped onto the field. The floodlights bathed the players in a harsh, brilliant glow, illuminating every bead of sweat, every tense muscle. The crowd—a mix of friends, family, and curious onlookers—clapped and cheered, their voices rising in a wave of excitement.

Ramesh's shoulders squared as he took his position. His focus was razor-sharp, his movements precise and deliberate. The whistle blew, and the game exploded into motion. The match unfolded like a symphony, a blend of speed, strategy, and raw athleticism. Ramesh owned the center field with a calculated precision that made him the linchpin of his team. His dribbles were effortless, his passes sharp and incisive. Weaving through defenders, he moved as though the ball were an extension of himself.

"Ramesh!" someone shouted, and he didn't hesitate. A quick pass, a swift turn, and the net rippled as the ball soared into the goal. Cheers erupted from his teammates, their voices briefly drowning out the night.

He scored again, another masterpiece of skill and timing. Yet, for all his brilliance, the opposing team from Bangalore was relentless. They exploited every gap, every moment of hesitation. The goals piled up, and by the time the final whistle blew, the scoreboard told the story of a hard-fought loss.

The aftermath of the game was quieter, the high-energy buzz replaced by the weight of exhaustion. Players collapsed onto the ground or leaned against the barriers, their shirts soaked with sweat. Some peeled them off, letting the night air cool their overheated bodies. Others grabbed their bags and slipped away into the shadows, eager to return to their lives beyond the turf.

Ramesh stood apart from the others, his expression unreadable. He didn't speak, didn't look back as he walked toward the alley, his footsteps echoing faintly in the distance.

"It was a good game," Amit said to the group, his voice filled with sportsmanlike cheer. "Well played, everyone. Hope to see you all again." He turned, waving at Ramesh's retreating figure. "Let's go, Ramesh."

But Ramesh was already gone, his silhouette swallowed by the night.

Surjeet stepped forward, still catching his breath. He called out after him, his voice laced with a mixture of concern and camaraderie. "Come by my place sometime, Ramesh."

Amit smiled at Surjeet and waved a quick goodbye, but it was clear Ramesh hadn't heard—or hadn't wanted to.

***

The house was silent except for the faint sizzling of onions hitting hot oil in the kitchen. The sound was rhythmic, almost soothing in its constancy, but it did little to ease Ramesh's turbulent thoughts. He worked with an efficiency born of routine, his hands chopping, stirring, and seasoning without hesitation. The kitchen's dim light pooled around him, isolating him in a small bubble of warmth and purpose. The aroma of frying spices filled the air, but Ramesh hardly noticed it. His mind was elsewhere, replaying fragments of the day—the game, the arguments, the faces of friends and strangers alike. Each memory felt like a shard of glass, sharp and unrelenting.

After setting the curry to simmer, he stepped into the bathroom, letting the steam from the cooking pot mingle with the cool air. The mirror greeted him with a reflection he didn't entirely recognize—a pale face, weary eyes, and a faint shadow of stubble along his jawline. He stared at it, searching for something in the depths of his own gaze, but all he found was an emptiness that made his chest tighten.

"I'm just an actor," he whispered to himself, a bitter smile creeping onto his lips. "A damn good one."

The words hung in the air, more an accusation than a statement. He leaned closer to the mirror, the cool surface fogging slightly from his breath. The light above flickered, casting erratic shadows across his features. The faint hum of the night crept through the walls, punctuated by the occasional distant horn from the street below.

Ramesh peeled off his shirt, revealing a lean torso marked with faint scars and the defined lines of someone who worked hard but never rested. His phone lay face-up on the sink, its flashlight casting a dim, synthetic glow that cut through the semi-darkness. He flipped the bathroom light off, letting the phone's glow dominate the room. The mirror reflected him now as a blurred silhouette, his body outlined in a hazy, yellowish light. The shadows behind him deepened, swallowing the edges of the room.

For a moment, he just stood there, staring at himself. His lips parted, and a sound escaped—low, uneven, almost primal.

"He heee heee..."

The sound grew, vibrating with an unnatural energy that made his own skin crawl. It wasn't a laugh or a sob, but something raw and feral, a voice that didn't feel entirely his own. He let it escape in bursts, testing its resonance in the stillness of the bathroom. It felt liberating, terrifying, and oddly comforting all at once.

"Ramesh!" His father's voice tore through the walls, breaking the fragile cocoon of sound he had created. "Ramesh, where are you? Come here for a minute!"

Ramesh's lips twitched, the strange sound dying in his throat. A thought surfaced, sharp and clear: *Can you hear him? That weak voice of your story, pulling you down. Suppress him. Suppress him and shine.*

"Ramesh, you freeloader!" His father's voice rose, laden with irritation. "How many times do I have to call you? Come here to—"

The rant trailed off as Ramesh flicked the light back on and headed out, his steps slow and deliberate. His feet felt heavy, as though weighed down by invisible chains, but he moved forward, dragging the weight behind him.

The dining area was modest but dominated by the oversized LCD TV mounted above the table. The faint flicker of a news channel cast shifting shadows across the polished surface of the table. His father lounged on the couch, one arm draped over the backrest, the other clutching the remote like a scepter. His posture radiated authority, a king surveying his dominion.

Ramesh entered, drying his damp hands with a towel. He tossed it onto a chair, his movements deliberately casual. "I was in the washroom," he said, his voice flat. "What?"

His father turned to him, his expression darkened by years of frustration. "You forgot to pull down the shutter today," he snapped. "And you didn't collect the money from the cashbox, you idiot."

Ramesh froze for a second, his mind racing to fill the gaps in his memory. "Oh, shit. Sorry. I'll go early tomorrow and deposit it."

"It's not just that!" His father's voice rose, filling the room like a storm. "You're too careless. Living like a king, watching movies all day! Mark my words—you'll repent the day I die."

The words hit Ramesh like a physical blow. His hand gripped the balcony door, his knuckles whitening against the handle. He pushed it open, letting in a rush of cold night air. It prickled against his skin, but he barely noticed. A bitter smile tugged at the corners of his mouth, his eyes fixed on the distant lights of the city.

"I've been waiting for that day," he muttered, his voice low but deliberate. "When a grumpy, old-minded sicko finally rests."

The words hung in the air, unchallenged. His father didn't hear them—or perhaps he chose not to.

The city's faint hum buzzed below. The sounds of distant car horns and the occasional bark of a stray dog blended into the static of the streetlights. Ramesh leaned against the balcony railing, his phone already in his hand. He scrolled through his contacts, his thumb hovering over a name before he pressed call.

"How are you, man?" Tony's voice crackled through the line, carrying a hint of suspicion.

"Fine," Ramesh replied. "Listen, I was thinking about buying some stuff from you. A little trip—how much?"

There was a pause on the other end. When Tony spoke again, his tone had sharpened. "Where are you now? Anyone around?"

"All alone. Don't worry."

"Buddy, I'm clean now," Tony said, his voice firm. "Don't mess with that shit anymore."

"I'll pay you double," Ramesh pressed, his voice carrying an edge of desperation.

Another pause, this one heavier.

"What happened to you?" Tony asked finally, his voice quieter now. "Everything okay? Listen, you're like my brother. I don't want what happened to me happening to you."

"Right, right. Sorry for asking," Ramesh said quickly, brushing off the concern. "Let's meet up sometime."

The silence stretched between them. Then, cautiously, Tony spoke again. "Can you lend me five thousand? Tomorrow morning."

Ramesh straightened slightly, the cold air biting into his skin. "Where?"

"Highway, near the rubber factory. And listen, buddy, don't mess this up."

"I'll see you tomorrow," Ramesh replied before hanging up. The screen went dark, leaving him alone with the city's muted symphony.

He stood there for a while, letting the chill seep into his bones. His thoughts churned, heavy and disjointed, like storm clouds gathering on the horizon. Finally, he turned and stepped back into the apartment, closing the balcony door behind him.

The room was dim, its corners swallowed by shadows. Ramesh crossed to his bed and sank onto the edge, his hands resting on his knees. He stared at the floor, the weight of the night pressing down on him. His mind buzzed with half-formed plans and lingering echoes of his father's words, each one cutting deeper than the last.

***

The tidy room stood like a shell, its outward neatness concealing the storm brewing within Ramesh. The old cupboard leaned tiredly against one wall, its wood worn and slightly warped by years of service. Beside it sat a small computer table, its surface cluttered with random papers and a blinking mouse. The double bed, unmade and chaotic, bore the scattered evidence of his turmoil—shirts, trousers, and crumpled socks lay like abandoned fragments of forgotten days.

Ramesh stood motionless in front of the mirror, his hands gripping the wooden frame as though it were the edge of a cliff. In his trembling fingers, he held a small photograph of his mother, its corners slightly frayed. Her gentle smile seemed to radiate warmth even through the worn, glossy paper. He stared at her face, his own reflection a stark contrast—tears carved deliberate trails down his cheeks, falling in heavy, unrelenting drops that splattered softly against the photograph's protective glass.

"You were the only one who believed in me," he whispered, his voice catching on the weight of the words. It cracked under the strain, raw and vulnerable, like a fragile thread threatening to snap. He held the photo closer to his chest for a moment, his fingers brushing against its surface as if trying to touch her through time.

With painstaking care, he placed the photograph on a nearby shelf, its position precise, almost reverential. He wiped his damp eyes with the edge of his sleeve, the gesture quick and almost angry, as if berating himself for his weakness. Turning away from the mirror, Ramesh stumbled backward onto the bed, the springs creaking softly under his weight. His head tilted upward, his gaze fixated on the blank expanse of the ceiling.

The room grew silent except for the sound of his uneven breathing. Then, from somewhere deep within, a melody began to stir.

"And I think it's gonna be a long, long time..." he murmured, his voice faltering as he began to sing Rocket Man. The tune emerged softly at first, the lyrics tumbling out in broken phrases, punctuated by long pauses. At times, his voice swelled, reaching for strength, but it often wavered, overcome by the tide of emotion threatening to drown him. He stopped mid-line more than once, closing his eyes tightly, as if shutting out the room around him might quiet the ache in his chest.

"I'm not the man they think I am at home... Oh, no, no, no..." he sang, the words carrying a strange resonance in the stillness of the room. The pauses between the lines stretched longer as the melody faltered, each gap filled with the unspoken weight of his thoughts. Ramesh's voice became a threadbare echo of itself, the raw edges of his grief bleeding into every note.

For a while, the song drifted into silence, leaving only the faint hum of the world outside. He stared at the ceiling as if searching for answers in its blankness, his lips trembling with words that refused to form. The photograph on the shelf caught the faint light from the window, its surface gleaming softly. His mother's image seemed to watch over him, her smile unwavering, an anchor amidst his storm.

Ramesh let out a long, shuddering breath, his chest rising and falling like waves crashing against a rocky shore. He clenched his fists, the fabric of the bedspread bunched tightly in his grip. Though the melody had ended, its essence lingered, wrapping around him like a fragile cocoon of memory and longing. For now, he let himself sink into the silence, each heartbeat a quiet reminder that he was still here, even if he didn't quite understand why.

***

Surjit stood on the balcony of his sprawling villa, the afternoon sunlight catching the sharp edges of his profile. The lush greenery below stretched out like a meticulously maintained carpet, each blade of grass as precise as a soldier in formation. The villa itself was a testament to his success, a tangible reminder of how far he'd come from the modest beginnings of his youth. Yet, at this moment, all of it felt hollow. His phone was pressed to his ear, his fingers tapping rhythmically on the metal railing. A faint smile played on his lips—not one of joy, but the kind you wear when you're trying to convince yourself that the lie you're telling might one day become the truth.

"You know, Meck," he said, his voice light but carrying an undercurrent of unease, "I thought that girl was into me."

From the other end came a burst of scratchy laughter, distant yet familiar. Meck's voice, muffled slightly by what Surjit imagined was the hum of an air conditioner in the background, replied with the kind of teasing certainty only an old friend could muster. "You thought so? Man, I'm sure about it. Just text her. She'd probably book a flight to India just to see you."

Surjit laughed, a short burst that sounded more like a release of air than genuine amusement. His eyes drifted down to the neatly trimmed lawn, where a gardener was methodically trimming the hedges. "Yeah, I don't know, man. Forget about it. Anyway, that Machegan guy really nailed it. The way he managed the Indian team... over-the-top hospitality. I think they keep him around for his charm more than anything else."

"True," Meck said, the sound of a can popping open in the background. "The guy's got charisma."

Before Surjit could reply, a voice called out from inside the house, cutting through the moment like a knife through silk. "Surjit! Come here for a minute. You've got a friend at the door."

He turned his head slightly, catching the reflection of his sister in the glass door that separated the balcony from the living room. Her arms were crossed, her expression neutral but tinged with impatience.

"Coming," he called back, his voice carrying an edge of reluctance. Into the phone, he said, "Hey, Meck, gotta go. We'll catch up later, yeah? Take care."

As he ended the call, a faint sigh escaped him, the kind that came not from physical exhaustion but from a weariness that ran far deeper. For a moment, he lingered on the balcony, his hand gripping the railing as if anchoring himself to the present. Then, with a deliberate slowness, he turned and walked inside.

His sister was waiting in the foyer, leaning against the staircase banister. She nodded toward the door. "It's Amit," she said simply, her tone devoid of any hint of surprise.

Surjit's reaction was immediate and familiar: a groan that seemed to originate from the very core of his being. Rolling his eyes, he muttered under his breath, "This guy..."

Before heading to the door, he detoured to the kitchen. The sound of water pouring from a pitcher into a glass filled the otherwise quiet space. He took a long drink, the cool liquid sliding down his throat, grounding him. Placing the empty glass on the counter with deliberate care, he made his way to the lobby.

Amit was standing awkwardly in the spacious entryway, his hands clasped in front of him like a schoolboy waiting outside the principal's office. The grandeur of the villa seemed to dwarf him, making his presence feel almost intrusive. Surjit spotted him through an open doorway and called out, his voice carrying a note of playful sarcasm. "Come on in, sir."

Amit looked up, startled. "This way?"

"Yes, yes," Surjit replied, motioning for him to follow.

The two settled in the guest room, a space designed for comfort but rarely used. Surjit sank into a plush armchair, his body relaxing into its embrace, while Amit perched uneasily on the edge of the sofa, his posture stiff. The air between them was thick with unspoken words, the kind of silence that presses down on you, demanding to be broken.

"How's it going, sir?" Surjit asked finally, his tone light but his eyes sharp. "What'll you have? Tea, coffee?"

Amit shook his head. "Actually, I'm full."

For a moment, he seemed to wrestle with his thoughts, his gaze darting around the room as if searching for the right words in the pattern of the wallpaper. Leaning forward slightly, he said, "Where's Auntyji?"

"She's at the neighbor's house," Surjit replied, sitting up a little straighter. "Did you get her reports?"

Amit hesitated, the pause stretching out just long enough to make Surjit's chest tighten with unease. When he finally spoke, his voice was measured but heavy. "Yes."

Surjit's eyes narrowed. "What happened?"

The question hung in the air, a live wire crackling with tension. Amit's shoulders sagged slightly, and he took a deep breath before answering. "She's got pancreatic cancer."

The words landed like a thunderclap, the weight of them reverberating through the room. Surjit's body went rigid, his breath catching in his throat. For a moment, he simply stared at Amit, as if hoping he'd heard wrong.

"The what?" he asked, his voice sharp and disbelieving.

"It's cancer," Amit repeated, quieter this time, the softness of his tone only amplifying the gravity of the statement.

Surjit's mind raced, his thoughts colliding in a chaotic tangle of fear and denial. "Show me the reports," he demanded, his voice rising.

"Why would I lie?" Amit shot back, a defensive edge creeping into his tone.

Surjit's voice cracked as he pressed on, desperation seeping into his words. "Motherfucker—this is curable, right?"

"Yes, yes, it is," Amit said quickly, his hands raised in a placating gesture. "But it requires surgery."

"And after the surgery? Will it all be clear? What are the risks?" Surjit's questions came in rapid succession, his words tumbling over each other in his urgency to understand.

"Listen to me," Amit said firmly, leaning forward and meeting Surjit's gaze. "I'll give you the doctor's number. He's one of the best—highly experienced in these cases. Call him. Ask him everything. Don't delay treatment. Please."

The plea in Amit's voice cut through Surjit's rising panic, grounding him just enough to let the reality of the situation sink in. For a moment, neither of them spoke, the silence heavy with the weight of what had just been revealed.

Finally, Amit broke the silence, his voice gentle but firm. "It's early stages, but cancer is cancer."

Surjit exhaled deeply, his body sinking back into the chair as if the weight of the news had physically pressed him down. "Oh my goodness," he murmured, his voice barely above a whisper. "This is... this is a big problem."

Amit stood, brushing his hands on his pants as if to shake off the heaviness of the conversation. "I should go now. Need to open the shop. If anything comes to mind, call me."

Surjit nodded, though he didn't rise to see him out. His eyes followed Amit as he walked to the door, his expression blank but for the faint twitch of his lips, a hint of something unspoken lingering in the air.

"Okay, we'll see then," Surjit said finally, more to himself than to Amit. "But this... this is serious."

"Don't worry," Amit said, pausing at the doorway and turning back. "It's curable."

With that, Amit left, his footsteps fading into the quiet of the house. Surjit sat alone in the guest room, the weight of the news settling over him like a suffocating blanket. His gaze drifted to the ceiling, his thoughts swirling in a maelstrom of fear, guilt, and determination. Somewhere in the distance, a clock chimed, marking the passage of time—a reminder that every moment now carried a new urgency.

The sunlight poured in through the half-drawn curtains of Surjit's spacious villa, painting golden streaks on the marble floor. The house was silent except for the faint hum of the air conditioner and the occasional rustle of leaves from the garden.

"Surjit!" his sister's voice cut through the haze. It was sharp and urgent, coming from another room. The sound jolted him, pulling him out of his reverie. With a groan, he straightened up, stretching his stiff shoulders, and trudged inside. Her tone wasn't one of casual conversation; it was heavier, more demanding. He braced himself for another storm.

He crossed the hallway with slow, deliberate steps, the polished tiles cold beneath his feet. Entering his sister's room, he was immediately hit by the icy blast of the air conditioner. The room was stark and modern, its minimalistic design almost clinical. The muted pastel walls contrasted sharply with the vibrant quilt wrapped tightly around her. She sat cross-legged on the bed, a picture of exhaustion and frustration, her face half-buried in the fabric.

"What happened?" Surjit asked, his voice low and tinged with annoyance. He shivered involuntarily, rubbing his arms for warmth. "And for God's sake, turn up the temperature. It's freezing outside."

Her eyes, dark and tired, fixed on him. "My life is so fucked up right now," she said flatly. There was no preamble, no softening of the blow.

He sighed, sinking into a chair near the window. "All our lives are," he replied, the weariness in his tone matching hers. He hesitated for a moment before continuing, his voice dropping even lower. "Amit told me some bad news."

She looked up, her expression shifting slightly, a flicker of curiosity breaking through her fatigue. "What bad news?"

"Mom's got pancreatic cancer," he said, the words heavy and deliberate, as though saying them aloud would make them less real.

For a moment, she didn't react. The silence stretched between them, thick and suffocating. Then she asked, "Then what?" Her tone was detached, almost clinical.

Surjit's brows knitted together in confusion. "Yes, yes, it is," he said, nodding slowly.

"Is it curable?" she asked, her voice calm but devoid of emotion.

"Yeah," he replied, though his tone lacked conviction. "Amit gave me the doctor's number. I'll talk to him about the details."

Her response was simple: "Oh no. This is serious." Her voice was flat, as if she were commenting on the weather.

Something in Surjit snapped. "Why are you acting so... artificial?" he demanded, his frustration bubbling to the surface. "This is Mom we're talking about!"

Her eyes narrowed, and her grip on the quilt tightened. "Artificial?" she shot back, her voice rising. "What do you mean? I'm depressed about my own life, and now you're dropping this on me. How am I supposed to react? Should I scream? Jump up and down? You tell me."

He threw up his hands in exasperation. "Just leave it. I'm not in the mood."

"You're never in the mood," she retorted, her voice dripping with sarcasm.

He shook his head, muttering under his breath, before changing the subject. "What were you going to tell me?" he asked, though his tone made it clear he wasn't particularly interested.

Her expression shifted again, this time to something more vulnerable. She hesitated, her lips pressing into a thin line before she finally spoke. "My marriage is on the edge," she said softly, almost as if she didn't want the words to be real.

Surjit blinked, caught off guard. "What is going on today?" he muttered, running a hand through his hair. "I can't process this. I don't even understand how this day's going to end."

She took a deep breath, her voice trembling slightly as she continued. "Rishab's having an affair," she said. "My friend saw him with a girl at the mall."

Surjit leaned back in his chair, rubbing his temples. "Jesus Christ," he muttered. "I don't know what to say. Just... give me a break."

"I just wanted you to know," she said, her tone defensive.

"Fine. You should tell me. But not now," he replied, waving a hand dismissively.

She frowned, her frustration mounting. "Well, I've noticed things. He hides stuff, sneaks out without reason, hesitates when I ask him things. And then one day..."

"Enough!" Surjit cut her off, his voice sharp. "I don't want the whole story. He's a son of a bitch. But right now, my head's spinning."

She looked away, her shoulders slumping. "Things are really that way now. I'm going to divorce him," she said quietly, the words heavy with finality.

Surjit shot to his feet, the chair scraping loudly against the floor. "I'm going out to the market," he said abruptly. "You want to come?"

She stared at him, incredulous. "Are you serious?"

"Dead serious," he replied, his tone flat.

"Get lost," she said, turning away from him.

He paused at the door, his hand on the frame. "And don't tell Mom anything," he said firmly before walking out. The door banged shut behind him, the sound echoing through the cold, silent house.

***

As he stepped outside, the crisp morning air hit him like a slap. He stuffed his hands into his pockets, his mind racing. The world felt too loud . Cars zipped past on the main road, their headlights piercing through the growing darkness. He wandered aimlessly, his feet carrying him without direction.

The day's revelations weighed heavily on him. His mother's illness, his sister's crumbling marriage—it was too much. He felt like he was drowning, each new piece of information a fresh wave pulling him under.

Surjit found himself at the local market, the bustle and noise providing a strange comfort. He walked through the crowded lanes, the smell of spices and street food filling the air. Vendors called out, their voices blending into a chaotic symphony. For a moment, he let himself get lost in the crowd, the anonymity a welcome escape.

He stopped at a tea stall, ordering a cup of chai. As he sipped the steaming beverage, he stared at the people around him. Families shopping for groceries, couples holding hands, children running and laughing

***

Later that evening, Ramesh parked his bike outside the theatre, rushing to secure his seat before the play began. Inside, the air buzzed with anticipation as the audience settled. The lights dimmed, and the story of Oedipus unfolded on the stage, the actors throwing themselves into their roles with exaggerated gestures and voices.

But Ramesh's mind wasn't on the tragedy before him. It was on Ridhi. The moment the applause ended, he moved backstage, searching the crowd.

There she was, laughing, glowing in the adoration of her friends and admirers. When their eyes met, she smiled—wide, confident, like nothing had ever gone wrong between them.

"Hello," she greeted. "How are you?"

"You were wonderful," he said, forcing a smile. "But the play was... okay."

"Are you sure about wonderful?" She laughed. "You might want to rethink that."

"Well," he said, his grin turning sharper, "it was horrific. Art-wise. The acting was so unauthentic."

Ridhi rolled her eyes, playful but pointed. "I've told you a thousand times—there's a difference between theatre acting and cinema acting. Maybe if you worked on your skills, you'd understand."

"Oh, I understand. I just don't want to waste my time with bad acting. What you're doing here is a hobby, not art."

"Sir Anthony Hopkins , feel free to join us," she shot back, grabbing his hand. Her sarcasm cut deep. "Teach us the masterclass we've all been waiting for."

"Do you want to catch a movie this weekend?" he asked abruptly.

She let go of his hand, laughing softly. "You've got nerve, you still think I'll give you that, After all the drama you pulled with your dad, you think we're going back to what we were?"

The words hung heavy in the air. Ridhi turned, walking away without waiting for an answer.

"Hey, listen," Ramesh called after her. "Do you think I'm a good person?"

She stopped, turning briefly to glance at him over her shoulder.

"I don't believe in anything you say." Her voice was steady, final.

And then she was gone.

Ramesh was a man on the edge, and it showed. His anger, his frustration, his discontent—it all bubbled under the surface, waiting to explode.

"I wasted my time on you," he muttered under his breath, storming out of the dimly lit theatre . His words weren't aimed at anyone in particular. Maybe himself. Maybe the world. He wasn't sure anymore. The streets outside the theatre were alive with noise, the hum of car engines mixing with the chatter of couples and groups spilling out of the other screens. He felt disconnected from it all, like a ghost floating through a crowd.

He didn't stop walking until he found himself outside a coffee shop. It was one of those clean, pretentious joints with baristas who wore aprons like they were surgeons. He hesitated at the entrance for a moment, looking at his reflection in the glass door. His hair was messy, his shirt wrinkled. He looked out of place.

Inside, the air smelled like ground beans and synthetic caramel. He ordered a latte, his voice almost too polite. "Sir, could I have a latte, please? Thank you, ma'am." He called everyone "sir" and "ma'am" like he was born into servitude, even though he hated the very idea of it.

While waiting for his drink, he studied the barista. Young, probably a college student, moving with precision and calm, despite the line of impatient customers. Ramesh couldn't help but wonder what kind of life the guy led.

"Yeah, Ramesh," he thought to himself, "you'll never make it in this world. You're not cut out for the grind. But these actors—these bad actors—they're worse. My idols? They're not theatre actors . They're people like Tony and me . I have all the charisma to hold an audience without even trying."

When his latte was ready, he slid 700 rupees across the counter as a tip. The barista stared at him, confused.

"You're a good actor," Ramesh said with a faint smile.

The barista stammered a thank-you, his bewildered expression lingering as Ramesh turned and left the shop. Outside, the evening was creeping in. The city buzzed with a burst of energy, and Ramesh felt it vibrating in his bones. He pulled out his phone and dialed Surjit.

"Hi, sir, how are you doing? It's me, Ramesh," he said, his tone cheerful, almost nonchalant.

Surjit's voice crackled on the other end, muffled by the background noise of a busy mall. "Well, good. Is this your number?"

"Nah, I borrowed a stranger's phone. My phone's battery died," Ramesh replied without missing a beat. "Honestly, I called for no serious reason. Just thought I'd talk to a rich guy and pick his brain about life."

Surjit's tone sharpened, irritation slipping through. "This is not the time for your antics. Mom has pancreatic cancer. I spoke to the doctor, and he said surgery is required. I'm not in the mood."

Ramesh paused, the teasing note in his voice fading. "Oh… sorry to hear that," he said, his tone softening. "Look, come over; we'll talk it out. The operation's not today, right?"

"Are you kidding me?" Surjit snapped, anger and disbelief cutting through his words. "Do you think this is some kind of joke? No, it's not today."

Ramesh's voice lightened again, though with a tinge of care. "And what are you doing right now?"

"I'm in the market," Surjit replied curtly.

A grin tugged at Ramesh's lips. "Now who's kidding who? You're in no mood, yet you're out shopping?"

"What do you want?" Surjit snapped, clearly losing patience.

Ramesh's tone turned serious. "I want to tell you something, but not over the phone."

"I don't have time to meet you," Surjit shot back.

"Well then," Ramesh said with mock determination, "I'll shop with you."

Surjit sighed, his frustration evident. "Is it something serious?"

"Very serious," Ramesh replied earnestly. "I need your advice. It's one of the biggest decisions of my life."

There was a pause before Surjit relented. "Fine, come to the mall."

"No, no, no. The mall's not safe," Ramesh said quickly. "Meet me near the Andheri cliff view. This isn't something I can discuss in a crowded or public place."

"What?" Surjit's confusion was clear. "I'm confused now. Are you mentally and physically okay?"

"Yes," Ramesh assured him. "But please don't tell anyone you're meeting me. I want to keep this private. It's a request."

"What happened?" Surjit's tone shifted, suspicion creeping in. "Are you caught up in some illegal trade or something?"

"No, no, nothing like that," Ramesh replied quickly. "It's personal. And one more thing... are you on your own vehicle?"

"Yeah, I'm in my car," Surjit confirmed.

"Okay, then. I'll pick you up from the mall," Ramesh said, his voice turning lighter again.

"Wait, wait. What's going on?" Surjit demanded.

"Nothing," Ramesh said with a chuckle. "I just want you to ride with me on my bike, like old times."

"And you'll drop me back at the mall? What the hell, Ramesh?"

"Okay, okay," Ramesh said, placating him. "Take your car and meet me by 7:00."

"If you promise to drop me back at the mall by 9:00, then come pick me up. It's already 6:00," Surjit said firmly.

"Alright, leaving now," Ramesh said, ending the call with a small sigh.

***

Ramesh rode his bike through the bustling streets, weaving through the traffic with practiced ease. He pulled to a stop at a roadside pan shop, dismounting with a deliberate air. His movements were unhurried as he purchased a packet of cigarettes, fumbling slightly with the cash as if distracted.

He lingered at the counter for a moment, leaning closer to the shopkeeper. "Do you have... um, a small knife?" he asked hesitantly, his voice low.

The shopkeeper's eyes narrowed with suspicion. "No," he replied curtly, shaking his head.

Ramesh sighed, disappointment flashing across his face. Without another word, he mounted his bike again and revved the engine. The machine roared to life as he sped off, heading to another shop down the street.

The sun dipped low on the horizon, casting long, golden shadows over the bustling streets. Ramesh pulled his bike into the parking lot of a modest restaurant near Gilbert Hill. The rumble of the engine faded as he double-locked the bike, his movements deliberate and calculated. He glanced around, ensuring no one was paying undue attention, before stepping toward Surjit, who stood nearby with a wary look on his face.

Surjit's eyes swept over the familiar surroundings. "It's been a while since I visited this place," he said, adjusting the sleeves of his jacket. He gestured toward the towering cliff ahead. "Ramesh, we'll get late if we climb up."

Ramesh waved a hand dismissively. "No problem, sir. Don't worry, you won't get late."

Surjit frowned but followed as Ramesh began the ascent up the hill. The path was uneven, littered with stray stones and overgrown grass. The climb was silent, punctuated only by the distant hum of city life and the occasional rustle of leaves. The temple perched atop the hill came into view as they approached, its bell echoing faintly through the evening air.

***

They found a spot near the temple, a secluded ledge with a panoramic view of the sprawling city below. Ramesh sat down first, leaning back on the cool stone surface. Surjit joined him hesitantly, sitting stiffly on the bench-like ledge. The golden hues of the setting sun bathed everything in a surreal glow.

Ramesh pulled a cigarette from a battered box, lighting it with a practiced flick. He took a long drag, exhaling the smoke into the fading light before turning to Surjit.

"So," Ramesh began, his tone casual, "you got any girlfriend or something?"

Surjit blinked, caught off guard by the question. "Seriously? That's what you want to talk about? My mother has cancer, Ramesh."

Ramesh closed his eyes, taking another drag from his cigarette. He exhaled slowly, the smoke curling upward. "She'll be fine. Physical ailments don't last for long."

Surjit's brows furrowed deeply. "It's cancer," he said, his voice tight with restrained anger.

Ramesh turned to look at him, his expression unreadable. He held Surjit's gaze for a moment, then looked away, as though words were unnecessary or irrelevant. The silence between them grew heavy. The rhythmic ringing of the temple bells and the low murmur of visitors provided a distant backdrop.

Finally, Surjit broke the silence. "What did you want to tell me?"

Ramesh flicked the ash from his cigarette, his eyes fixed on the horizon. "Me and Ridhi are planning for a marriage."

Surjit's expression softened slightly, though skepticism lingered. "What? Fantastic! Ridhi, that actress, right? I heard you guys broke up long ago. Have you told Uncle ji?"

Ramesh sighed. "The problem is, she doesn't like me."

Surjit's patience was wearing thin. "Now tell me what you really want to say. Please. I'm not in the mood."

Ramesh took another drag from his cigarette, the embers glowing faintly in the dimming light. "How do you see life?"

Surjit groaned. "I told you, I'm not in the mood."

Ramesh chuckled softly, shaking his head. "Well, then you're not interested in life. I love her. She's one of my kind, but I sabotaged myself. I want to make her believe that my life is empty without her." He paused, his voice taking on a quieter, almost reflective tone. "My father will soon die naturally. I don't want to run the shop for long. I want that girl to guide me, but she's simply not interested in me. I want to do something."

Surjit sighed deeply, the weight of the day pressing on him. "Well, honestly, today is not a good day to ask me anything about relationships. Especially."

Ramesh leaned forward, his cigarette dangling between his fingers. "But I want to do something right now. I always wanted to be a movie star. Movie stars don't sit like this."

Surjit's lips twitched in a faint, humourless smile. "Then try hard, buddy. That's all it takes."

Ramesh's eyes narrowed slightly. "I'm not a labourer like you."

Surjit's face hardened. "I think that's the only problem."

Ramesh studied him for a moment before speaking. "Can I ask you a question?"

Surjit glanced at his watch. "But after that, I need to get up and head home. So make it quick."

Ramesh's voice was low, almost a whisper. "Do you believe in me?"

Surjit's response was immediate, sharp. "No. You're just getting insane. You say one thing and do another. How can somebody believe in you? Let's go now. It's getting late."

Ramesh's jaw tightened, his fists clenching at his sides. He took a deep breath, forcing a smile. "Yeah, you're right. I'm just a pretender."

His eyes darted around, scanning the area. The temple bells continued their rhythmic toll, and the chatter of visitors grew distant. The fading light cast long shadows across the rocky ledge. Sensing the moment, Ramesh acted swiftly.

In a sudden motion, he pulled a rope from his jacket and looped it around Surjit's neck. Surjit's hands flew to his throat, his eyes wide with shock and terror as he struggled to free himself. Ramesh tightened the rope, his knuckles white with effort, and pressed his hand against Surjit's face, muffling his desperate cries.

The struggle was brief but brutal. Surjit thrashed, his legs kicking against the rocky ground. Ramesh's movements were methodical, his face eerily calm. As Surjit's resistance weakened, Ramesh reached into his pocket and pulled out the knife. Without hesitation, he drew it across Surjit's throat, the blade slicing through with a sickening ease. Blood gushed from the wound, pooling on the stone and dripping over the edge.

***

Surjit's body convulsed violently before going still. The only sound was the distant hum of the city and the faint ringing of the temple bells.

Ramesh leaned in close, his breath visible in the cool evening air. He stared at Surjit's lifeless face, his expression a mixture of fascination and detachment.

"They say it very right," Ramesh murmured. "No money can literally buy you another second on Earth."

He stood up, pulling out a small bottle of sanitiser from his jacket. Carefully, he wiped the knife clean, ensuring no trace of blood remained. He then rummaged through Surjit's pockets, retrieving his phone and wallet. Without a backward glance, Ramesh walked away, his steps measured and deliberate.

***

Ramesh stumbled back towards the mall parking lot, his face a map of quiet frustration. The sim card from Surjit's phone was already in his palm, cracked into uselessness. He took a quick glance around—just a handful of distracted shoppers milling about, faces aglow from their phones. Without ceremony, he flung the shattered sim into a nearby drain. Surjit's wallet followed soon after, landing with a soft thud against the pavement before he gave it a casual kick into the same grate. He didn't look back. He never did.

***

Night folded itself thickly over the small apartment, its dim corridors lit by the flickering glow of a TV. Ramesh emerged from the bathroom, a threadbare towel slung over one shoulder. The damp air clung to him as he padded toward the lobby, where his father sat glued to the Kapil Sharma Show, his laughs soft and infrequent, like they were only half-earned.

Ramesh moved toward the kitchen, pulling together a plate of food with a mechanical efficiency. The clink of utensils against ceramic punctuated the muffled sound of studio laughter. He settled onto the sofa, his dinner balanced on his lap, the smell of curry sharp and inviting.

For a moment, neither man spoke. Silence lingered in the room, thick and heavy.

His father broke it first.

"Where you got this curry from?"

"Ordered it," Ramesh replied, not looking up.

His father leaned forward, squinting at the plate like it held secrets.

"Looking nice."

"Taste and tell me," Ramesh said, absently tearing at a piece of roti.

"I mean, not that much greasy," his father muttered, taking a tentative bite. He chewed slowly, savouring it, then nodded in approval.

"Oh hoo, delectable. I enjoyed it."

Ramesh smirked faintly, his eyes shifting toward the TV. "Now the craze for this show is dying out. Let's see what else is on."

He picked up the remote, switching over to YouTube. The opening notes of *The Godfather* rolled out from the speakers, filling the room with gravitas.

His father sighed heavily, an exaggerated gesture meant to provoke.

"These movies ruin your mind. Watch something useful sometimes, like the news."

Ramesh chuckled, low and dry.

"Tell me, what do you use news for?"

His father paused, searching for a retort, then said, abruptly, "Well, news keeps us aware of everything happening around us. In actual."

"In actual?" Ramesh echoed, his smirk widening. "Father, you know what's actual? A lie. News is for peasants, people who want rulers of different kinds to provoke them."

His father leaned back, crossing his arms. "And movies are the truth?"

"Not the truth," Ramesh admitted, "but they improve our personality."

"Then I love to be a peasant," his father shot back, raising his chin slightly in defiance.

The conversation was interrupted by the shrill ring of Ramesh's phone. He muted the TV with a quick press of the remote and answered, his tone shifting into something softer, almost polite.

"No, Aunty, what happened?"

There was a pause, a faint crackle of static on the other end. "Ok...hm...ok. I was at the theatre. Is he not picking calls? Ok, well, if I get to know anything, I'll call. Don't worry; he must be stuck somewhere."

He hung up, the lightness in his face vanishing.

His father squinted at him, concern creeping into his voice. "What happened?"

Ramesh sighed, running a hand through his hair. "Surjit isn't picking calls. He hasn't come home yet. Aunty ji is worried."

"This is something to be worried about," his father said, glancing at the clock. "It's around 10:30 now."

"Maybe his phone battery's dead," Ramesh suggested, though his voice lacked conviction. "I don't know."

"Well, call her after an hour or two."

"Ok." Ramesh stood, brushing crumbs from his shirt. "I'm going downstairs for a walk. Please clean the dishes."

"Shame on you," his father grumbled, grabbing the remote. "Can I change the channel now?"

"Yeah, sure. See what suits you."

"Go away, you fucker," his father snapped, his tone carrying a strange warmth beneath the insult.

Ramesh shot him a sulky look but said nothing, disappearing slowly into the shadows of the lobby. Behind him, the TV flickered, switching back to the comfortable absurdity of comedy, as if it could drown out the small, sharp worries hanging in the air.

The night outside was still, but it carried the kind of weight that pressed against the chest, an unspoken tension that followed Ramesh like a second shadow as he walked away.

***

Next day , The morning sun rose sluggishly, its pale light filtering through the heavy curtains of the small living room. It was a quiet morning, almost unnaturally so, as though the world were holding its breath. Ramesh sat at the dining table, absently stirring a cup of tea that had long since gone cold. His father, was in the adjacent room, flipping through a newspaper, the crinkling of pages the only sound breaking the stillness.

It was then that the phone rang, its shrill tone slicing through the calm like a knife. Father hurried to answer, his voice calm but curious. As he listened, his expression shifted. The lines on his weathered face deepened, his shoulders stiffened, and his grip on the receiver tightened.

When he finally put the phone down, his hands trembled slightly. "Ramesh," he called, his voice barely above a whisper. "It's Surjit... he..." father paused, as though the words were too heavy to utter. "He's gone."

Ramesh looked up, startled. "Gone? What do you mean?"

"Dead. They found him by the river. There was... blood. A lot of it." father's voice cracked as he spoke.

For a moment, the world seemed to tilt. Ramesh's chest tightened, but he felt strangely detached. "No," he muttered, shaking his head. "That can't be right." Yet, deep down, he knew it was.

The father and son dressed hurriedly, their movements mechanical, and made their way to Surjit's home. The streets seemed unusually busy for such an early hour, as though the city itself was unsettled by the tragedy.

When they arrived, the house was filled with mourners. A heavy pall hung in the air, broken only by the sound of muffled sobs. Surjit's mother sat on the floor in a corner, her face buried in her hands. Her frail frame shuddered with the force of her grief. Arun approached her cautiously, his own face a mask of sorrow.

"How did this happen?" Arun asked softly, his voice laden with sympathy.

Surjit's mother lifted her face, tears streaking down her cheeks. She tried to speak but choked on her words. Finally, she managed to whisper, "They said... they found him... near the river... so much blood..." Her words dissolved into sobs.

Ramesh stood behind his father, his fists clenched at his sides. The sight of Surjit's mother's anguish was unbearable, and yet, he couldn't bring himself to move. He felt a strange mixture of emotions swirling within him — disbelief, guilt, and something darker that he couldn't quite name.

Among the mourners, a few police officers stood quietly, their presence adding an ominous weight to the room. They were here to investigate, murmuring to one another in hushed tones as they observed the scene. One of them caught Ramesh's eye briefly, his expression unreadable. The very thought that someone might have killed Surjit sent a shiver down Ramesh's spine.

"Surjit was my best friend," Ramesh declared suddenly, his voice louder than he intended. Heads turned to look at him, some with curiosity, others with sympathy. He raised his hands dramatically as though addressing an unseen audience. "He just came back from the U.S. We were planning a trip together. A small one. Just to catch up, you know? And now..." His voice cracked, but he pressed on, his tone veering into something almost theatrical. "Now he's gone. Life always hits hardest when we... when we think we've finally settled things."

His father placed a hand on his shoulder, grounding him. "Ramesh," father said gently, his voice heavy with caution.

Ramesh nodded quickly, brushing at his face as though wiping away tears. "I need some air," he muttered and pushed his way through the crowd.

Outside, the air was crisp but offered little comfort. Ramesh walked aimlessly, his steps uneven. He found himself standing by a street cobbler, a man whose wrinkled hands worked tirelessly as though oblivious to the world's tragedies. For some reason, the sight undid Ramesh. He leaned against a nearby wall and let the tears come, silent and unrelenting. He watched the cobbler's hands move with practiced precision, a stark contrast to the chaos swirling within him. There was something profoundly grounding about the man's calm focus, and yet it made Ramesh feel even more lost.

After what felt like an eternity, Ramesh straightened and wiped his face. The weight of the day bore down on him, but he steeled himself and returned to his father, who was waiting by the gate. Together, they made their way home, their steps heavy with grief. Neither spoke during the journey. Words seemed unnecessary, even intrusive, in the face of such loss.

Ramesh sat in his shop, drumming his fingers on the counter. The shelves, stacked with mundane essentials, seemed to mock him with their monotony. The fluorescent lights buzzed faintly overhead, casting a dull glow on the rows of soap bars, toothpaste tubes, and packets of rice. His eyes wandered aimlessly across the shop, landing on Sumit Ji, the middle-aged man who worked for long as his assistant.

"Sumit Ji," Ramesh called out, his voice carrying a tinge of irritation, "watch over the shop. I'm going out for a pan."

Sumit Ji looked up from the newspaper he was reading, gave a nod, and went back to flipping pages. He didn't question Ramesh; he knew better.

The air outside felt thick, warm, and slightly polluted. Ramesh loosened his collar and crossed the street to the pan shop. The shop itself was a modest affair—a small, brightly lit stall with colourful jars of betel leaves, tobacco packets, and candy stacked precariously on its counter. The vendor, a wiry man with a pencil moustache, greeted Ramesh with a slight nod.

"One meetha pan," Ramesh said, leaning against the counter.

The vendor got to work, his fingers moving deftly as he assembled the pan. Ramesh watched, half-interested, while the sounds of the street filled his ears—scooters whizzing by, the occasional honk, a woman haggling loudly with a vegetable vendor.

He took the pan, placed it in his mouth, and let the burst of sweetness flood his senses. It was a small pleasure, but it grounded him.

As he stood there, chewing absentmindedly, something unusual caught his attention. Across the street, near a small jewelry store, a group of men huddled suspiciously. They were dressed too casually for the area—sloppy jeans, oversized shirts, and caps pulled low over their faces. Ramesh squinted, his instincts kicking in.

The huddle broke, and two of the men moved toward the jewelry store's entrance. One stayed outside, pacing nervously and glancing up and down the street.

"Looks like trouble," the pan vendor muttered, following Ramesh's gaze.

Ramesh didn't respond. His jaw slowed its chewing as he watched the two men disappear into the store. Through the glass, he could see a commotion brewing—arms waving, the store clerk backing up, his hands raised.

The pacing man outside fidgeted more now, clearly on edge. Ramesh felt his pulse quicken. He wasn't the kind of man who got involved in things like this. Life becomes simpler when you stayed in your lane, but something about the scene gnawed at him.

Then it happened. A loud crash came from inside the store—a showcase shattered, its glass spilling like jagged water onto the floor. The pacing man outside stiffened, then turned to look directly at Ramesh.

Their eyes locked for a moment, and Ramesh froze. He didn't know what he expected—a confrontation, maybe. But the man turned away quickly, shouting something into the store.

Ramesh's heart pounded in his chest as he saw the men rush out, carrying bags that jingled with stolen goods. They bolted down the street, weaving through pedestrians, disappearing into the maze of alleys.

«Police'll never catch them," the pan vendor said bitterly, shaking his head.

Ramesh stood there, rooted to the spot, his pan half-chewed and forgotten in his mouth. He felt a strange mix of fear and exhilaration. For a moment, his dull, predictable life had collided with something raw and dangerous.

He spat out the pan and turned back toward his shop.

Sumit Ji looked up as Ramesh walked in, his face pale and drawn.

"What happened ? did they scamper away ?  " Sumit Ji asked, sensing something was off. " that was terrible;  people s courage got exhilarated nowadays "  he continued .

"Nothing , it was funny to watch silly drama " Ramesh muttered, taking his place behind the counter. But his hands trembled slightly as he reached for a cigarette.

Lighting it, he took a long drag and stared out of the shop's front window. The city moved on, indifferent and chaotic, but Ramesh couldn't shake the feeling that something had shifted, however small, in the fabric of his mind .

For now, though, he buried the internal numbness . There were shelves to stock and customers to serve. The monotony would wrap itself around him again, suffocating but familiar. He exhaled a cloud of smoke and tried to let it go.

***

Day after , afternoon sunlight seeped through the narrow gaps in the window, highlighting the cracks on the walls of Ramesh's tiny rented room. He stood in front of a rust-streaked mirror, tugging at the knot of his tie for the third time. The faded blue fabric refused to cooperate, bunching awkwardly at his throat. Ramesh sighed, his breath fogging up the glass for a moment. The city of Mumbai, famed for its sprawling dreams and ceaseless energy, felt unusually oppressive today.

His room was a cramped square of peeling paint and mismatched furniture, far removed from the gleaming offices he'd once pictured himself working in. A solitary poster of a serene Himalayan landscape hung on the wall—a stark contrast to the chaos outside. The poster was a gift from his sister, who often joked that Ramesh needed to find peace, if not in life, then at least in a picture.

"Its action time ," he murmured, forcing a weak smile at his reflection. His voice lacked conviction.

Grabbing his worn leather bag, Ramesh stepped into the streets of a Mumbai morning. The air was thick with a cocktail of smells—freshly fried vada pav, exhaust fumes, and the faint tang of salt carried in from the side  shops. The sidewalks bustled with life: chai vendors shouting to customers, hawkers arranging their wares, and the occasional stray dog weaving through the chaos.

The interview was at a mid-sized sales company in Bandra complex , a neighbourhood known for its blend of corporate ambition and local vibrancy. Ramesh took a crowded local train, holding on to the overhead grip as the compartments swayed and jolted. The rhythmic clatter of the tracks did little to calm his nerves.

When he finally reached the office building, its glass façade gleamed under the sun, reflecting the relentless motion of the streets below. Ramesh stared at his reflection in the towering windows, adjusting his tie once more. The building's polished exterior contrasted sharply with the storm of emotions raging inside him.

Inside, the air was crisp and cold, a stark reminder of how far he was from the world he aspired to join. A receptionist with a perfectly curated smile directed him to the waiting area. As he sat, his palms began to sweat, and he rehearsed his answers under his breath, hoping they sounded confident.

"Ramesh Sharma?" The receptionist's voice jolted him.

He walked into the interview room with shaky confidence. Three people sat across a polished wooden table: a stern-faced man in his fifties, a younger woman scribbling notes on a clipboard, and a man in his thirties who seemed more interested in his phone than the proceedings. The room smelled faintly of coffee and expensive cologne.

The questions began innocuously enough. "Tell us about yourself," the older man said, his voice measured.

Ramesh recited his practiced answer, mentioning his modest educational background and his determination to prove himself. But soon, the tone shifted.

"Describe a time you closed a deal under pressure," the older man asked, leaning back in his chair and folding his arms.

Ramesh hesitated. His resume was a patchwork of odd jobs, none of which fit neatly into corporate expectations. He fumbled through a story about persuading a hesitant customer at a local electronics shop, but the man's raised eyebrow betrayed his skepticism.

The younger woman scribbled something on her clipboard, her expression unreadable. The executive on his phone glanced up briefly, his face a mix of boredom and mild disdain.

By the time the interview ended, Ramesh's hopes had sunk to the soles of his scuffed shoes.

"We'll get back to you," the woman said, her tone polite but final.

Ramesh nodded, forcing a smile he didn't feel. Outside, the noise of Mumbai hit him like a wave. He walked aimlessly, the city's chaos blurring into a dull hum in his ears. His thoughts spiraled: inadequacy, anger, and desperation clawed at his mind.

When exhaustion overtook him, he hailed an autorickshaw to take him back to his room. The driver, a wiry man with a scruffy beard, muttered complaints as soon as they hit the infamous Mumbai traffic.

"These politicians don't care about us," the driver said, his voice sharp with frustration. "The cost of everything is rising. How are we supposed to survive?"

Ramesh stared out at the blinking city lights, his silence a fragile dam holding back the storm within.

"They're all the same," he muttered eventually, more to himself than the driver.

"Exactly!" the driver exclaimed, emboldened. "They don't care about people like you and me. We're nothing to them."

The man's incessant rant grated on Ramesh's frayed nerves. By the time they reached a deserted stretch of road, the tension had built to an unbearable peak.

What happened next felt like a blur, a series of disconnected moments that Ramesh couldn't fully piece together later. A flash of anger, a scuffle, and then the driver's lifeless body crumpled on the ground. The world seemed to pause, the city's distant hum replaced by the deafening thud of Ramesh's heartbeat.

His hands trembled as he dragged the body to the roadside woods and removed stains from the knife when he realised that he slaughtered a rickshaw wala . The trees cast long shadows under the dim glow of distant streetlights, their branches swaying like silent witnesses. Ramesh's breath came in short, shallow gasps. When he finally let go of the body, a wave of numbness washed over him.

"That was silly " he said .

***

The next day , in the late afternoon sun draped itself over the old, weathered school building as the car pulled into the driveway. Amit's hands were steady on the wheel, but his mind was distant, focused on picking up his little brother. Beside him, Ramesh sat in a rare, contemplative silence, his eyes fixated on the faded red bricks of the structure that had shaped, and perhaps scarred as tilted his head to a side and twisted his lips , bit it a little .

"You're quiet," Amit remarked, glancing sideways as he parked.

Ramesh didn't respond immediately. His gaze lingered on the cracked basketball court, the chain-link fence that rattled in the wind, and the faint chatter of children playing in the distance. Something about being here, in this place, scratched at the edges of his memory—a place he had once hated to revisit, either physically or mentally.

"It hasn't changed much, has it?" Amit continued, stepping out of the car. Amit voice was light, almost nostalgic, but it only served to deepen the weight pressing down on Ramesh's chest. He remained seated, his fingers gripping the armrest tightly as his mind spiraled back to a time he had buried deep.

It started with the classroom—a cramped, sunlit space that always felt too small, too suffocating. The smell of chalk dust lingered in his nostrils as if it had never left. He remembered sitting in the back, hunched over his desk, trying to make himself invisible. But no matter how much he shrank, he couldn't escape their eyes. The teacher's voice boomed in his ears, louder than the murmurs of his classmates.

"Ramesh! Stand up!"

His eleven-year-old self obeyed, trembling as he rose to his feet. She embarrassed in front of everyone again , sitting at her chair , her face twisted with disdain.

"Why can't you get anything right? How many times do I have to explain this?" she snapped, pointing at the half-crossed scribbles on the his notebook . "Even a  4 th  standard student here understands better than you."

The awkwardness erupted around him, sharp and unforgiving. It was a glimpse  he would never forget— not because it hurt, but because it fuelled something life Threatening inside him. That was the day he first felt it: the deep desolation bubbling beneath the surface, the desire to lash out, to make the world feel the same air that was  inflicted on him.

But the worst came later. During recess, as he sat alone under the tree, a group of boys approached. Their leader, a broad-shouldered boy named Arjun, smirked as he towered over Ramesh.

"Hey lunatic ," Arjun began, snatching the tattered book from Ramesh's hands. "Trying to eat ? Like it'll make you any less harsh ."

later , at closing time , in bus the same guy scuffled with ramesh for a seat to secure beside diver ' s seat and  the words from boys s mouth amplified and echoing in ramesh s skull. Something snapped. Before he realised what he was doing, Ramesh grabbed the steel ruler from his bag and swung it with all his might. The edge of the ruler tore across Arjun's cheek, leaving a jagged, bloody gash. Arjun screamed, clutching his face, and the laughter dissolved into panicked cries.

The aftermath was chaos. The headteacher's office smelled of old varnish and disappointment as Ramesh's parents were summoned next day . His father stood stiffly, arms crossed and face unreadable, while his mother was listening to every line of teacher carefully . Parents grabbed chairs .whereas ramesh was watching this rendezvous from a distant sight , through  the office half opened door .

"What's wrong with him ?" the headteacher demanded, her voice a mix of anger and exasperation. "Why can't he behave like a decent  child?"

"He's just a kid ," mother said. "He didn't mean it. He gets scared all the time , that's all."

"Scared?" the headteacher scoffed. "This isn't fear. It's violence that he committed many times . You are teacher yourself , you know how other parents would react to this  . If this continues, he won't have a future in our school or may be outside ."

And after sensing the end of the conversation ramesh nervously turned from lurching position and scampered downstairs to attend morning assembly

That night, Ramesh overheard his parents arguing. His father's voice was cold and sharp, accusing, while his mother's was soft, pleading.

"He's not like other kids," his father said. "He's weak. Mentally, physically. If we coddle him, he'll never grow up."

"He's our son," his mother replied. "He needs love, not scolding."

Ramesh clung to her words, her warmth, her embrace. She was the only one who ever made him feel safe. But that safety was short-lived. One fateful evening, she boarded the school bus after finishing her shift at work. She never came home. The accident made the news for days, the images of twisted metal and shattered glass seared into his mind.

"Ramesh?" Amit's voice pulled him back to the present. He blinked, realising he was still in the school. His hands were trembling now, his breath shallow.

"You okay?" Amit asked, his tone cautious.

Ramesh forced a nod, swallowing the lump in his throat. "Yeah. Just... memories."

Amit hesitated, sensing the weight of his words. "Good ones?"

Ramesh's lips curved into a bitter smile. "Not exactly."

"Let's just get your brother and leave," Ramesh muttered, his voice low.

Amit glanced at him but said nothing and they made their way out .

***

When Ramesh returned home, the evening lay heavy with a suffocating stillness. Shadows cloaked the house in a shroud of foreboding, and a dim, flickering glow from the living room television cast eerie, restless figures upon the walls. Each shadow seemed alive, as if bearing witness to the night's grim unfolding. Ramesh paused at the threshold, a solitary figure standing amidst the weight of an invisible storm.

Inside, his father sat in his customary chair, a once-proud figure now diminished by the relentless march of age and illness. His form was hunched, frail, and every rasping breath betrayed the ceaseless war within his lungs. The sound filled the room, a testament to his suffering. And there, on the coffee table, lay the inhaler—an object so small yet so powerful, a symbol of fragile hope cruelly placed just out of reach.

"Ramesh," his father's voice emerged, a faint and tremulous whisper that seemed to rise from the depths of his despair. "Bring me the inhaler."

Ramesh's silhouette loomed in the doorway, motionless, his face obscured by the interplay of shadow and light. For a moment, he remained rooted there, his expression veiled in an impenetrable mask of indifference. His father's hand quivered as it reached out, trembling with an urgency that only the imminence of death can inspire.

"Please," the old man croaked, the plea barely audible yet heavy with desperation.

Time itself seemed to hesitate as Ramesh finally stepped forward. His movements were deliberate, each step echoing like the tolling of a bell. He reached the coffee table, his gaze fixed on the inhaler, as though it were an artefact of a bygone age, foreign and strange. Turning it over in his hands, he examined it with a curious detachment, as if weighing its significance against some unspoken measure.

For a fleeting instant, his father's eyes flickered with the faintest glimmer of hope. But hope is a fragile thing, easily snuffed out. With an almost ceremonial precision, Ramesh placed the inhaler back on the table and turned away. Behind him, his father's rasping breaths grew fainter, each one more laboured than the last, until they ceased altogether. The room fell into a profound silence, broken only by the faint hum of the television.

For a long moment, Ramesh stood still, his back to the lifeless form of his father. Then, he turned and knelt beside the chair. He wrapped his arms around the still-warm body of his lifeless father , holding it in a silent embrace that spoke of emotions too complex and tangled to name. It was a gesture of longing, of hidden tears , of something far beyond simple grief. When he finally released him, Ramesh arranged the body carefully, ensuring his father sat in peaceful repose, as if merely resting.

Agitation consumed him as he stumbled toward the kitchen. His bare feet faltered on the cold floor, and he reached for a glass with trembling hands. He filled it with water and drank deeply, the liquid coursing through him like a balm, though it did little to soothe the storm within. He leaned against the counter, staring into the dim void of the room.

At last, he retreated to his bedroom, closing the door with a deliberate finality. The house's stillness seemed to magnify the sound, reverberating in the emptiness. Ramesh sat on the edge of his bed, his head in his hands, wrestling with emotions he could neither name nor suppress. The night stretched on, oppressive and endless.

The morning brought with it the murmurs of the neighbourhood. Word of his father's passing had spread, and clusters of neighbours gathered outside, their voices low and tinged with speculation.

"A heart attack," someone said. "He'd been unwell for so long."

"Such a shame," another added. "And Ramesh... such a quiet boy. Who will take care of him now?"

Inside, Ramesh wore his mask well. He moved among the mourners with practiced solemnity, his face a carefully crafted tableau of grief. He bowed his head in gratitude at their condolences, his voice steady as he thanked them for their kindness. To all appearances, he was the devoted son, mourning the loss of his only family. No one questioned him; why would they? Ramesh had always been the quiet, unassuming one, the dutiful son who bore his burdens without complaint.

***

Days went by and then after about a month , he met Amit at their usual tea stall. The air was thick with the aroma of chai and the cacophony of city life. The shopkeeper, familiar with their routine, greeted them with a nod and handed them steaming glasses of tea. They sat at their usual rickety table, the world bustling around them.

For a time, they sipped in silence, the kind born of years of companionship. But Ramesh broke it with a sentence that fell like a stone into still waters.

"I did it," he said, his voice calm and unyielding.

Amit looked up, startled. "Did what?"

"I killed him," Ramesh replied, his tone matter-of-fact. "My father. And Surjit."

Amit laughed nervously, the sound brittle and uncertain. "You're joking," he said. "Don't mess around like that."

"I'm not joking," Ramesh said, leaning forward. His eyes bore into Amit's, unflinching and devoid of humour. "I killed them both. I watched them die."

The laughter died on Amit's lips. "Ramesh," he said cautiously, "you've been under a lot of stress. Maybe... maybe you're imagining things."

"It's not stress," Ramesh snapped, his voice sharp. "Don't dismiss this as some kind of breakdown. Something has changed in me. I don't feel anything anymore—not guilt, not fear. Nothing."

Amit's expression shifted from concern to fear. "You're scaring me," he admitted, his voice barely audible.

"You should be scared," Ramesh said, a bitter smile twisting his lips. "Because I don't know what's going to happen next."

"Nothing will happen next," Amit said firmly, placing his hands on Ramesh's shoulders. "Be calm. Gather yourself. I'm with you."

Ramesh shook his head. "But I'm not with me," he said softly, his voice breaking for the first time.

A long silence fell between them, heavy with unspoken truths. Finally, Ramesh asked, "Do you believe me, Amit? Do you trust me?"

Amit hesitated, his fear and loyalty warring within him. Slowly, he tightened his grip on Ramesh's shoulders and met his gaze. "I do," he said, though his voice trembled. And in that moment, both men knew the world they had known was irreversibly changed.

***

Later that day : dim lights of the theatre painted shadows along the walls, faint and flickering as if the room itself were alive, breathing along with the audience. The faint scent of stale popcorn and varnished wood hung in the air. In the last row of the vast auditorium sat Ramesh, his posture rigid, shoulders hunched forward, as though trying to disappear into the seat. Around him, bursts of laughter rolled like waves, a joyous tide engulfing the room. The comedy play on stage was doing its job well—its performers timing their lines with precision, their movements crafted to evoke delight.

Yet, Ramesh's face remained unmoved. His lips, pressed into a thin, bloodless line, refused to participate in the merriment. His dark eyes, shadowed by a sleepless night, were locked on the stage, not with interest but as if shackled there by some unseen force. His jaw tightened with every peal of laughter, every eruption of applause, until his discomfort seemed palpable, a visible thing.

From afar, the play looked seamless, an illusion of effortless humor. Performers danced in exaggerated motions, their quips met with uproarious reactions. The audience around Ramesh swayed in delight, leaning into one another, their faces lit with joy. But Ramesh felt none of it. The laughter grated on him. It echoed in his head, twisted and grotesque. Was this how others felt happiness—so easy, so immediate? It was incomprehensible to him. The stage blurred in his vision, the actors transforming into grotesque caricatures.

The curtains fell, and the applause rose like a thunderclap. Ramesh remained still, a ghost in a sea of animation.

***

Outside the theatre, he waited. His hands were in his pockets, his shoulders drawn close to his body as though bracing against a chill that wasn't there. The noise of departing patrons surrounded him, their animated conversations cutting through the silence of his thoughts. The streetlights above flickered, casting sporadic beams across the pavement, and the world felt stark and artificial.

Ridhi appeared, her movements brisk but distracted. She had always carried a certain air of composure, even in the most mundane of situations. She stopped short when she saw him, tilting her head slightly, her expression caught between warmth and something more cautious.

"How are you?" he asked, his voice low, almost drowned out by the passing crowd.

"Good, good..." Ridhi replied, her gaze darting past him. "Wait, Ramesh, I'll come back to you in a few minutes. I need to head backstage."

She gave him a quick smile—kind, obligatory—before disappearing into the throng. For a moment, he remained frozen, as if unsure what to do with himself. Then, slowly, he turned. His feet moved hesitantly at first, then with purpose, carrying him away from the crowd and the theatre.

The cold weight in his chest grew heavier with every step. He had tried to muster a smile, but it had felt like an alien act, foreign and awkward. His phone buzzed in his pocket, and he pulled it out, glancing at the screen before answering.

"Hello?"

"Ramesh," Ridhi's voice came through, firm yet tinged with concern. "Where are you?"

"I'm just outside," he said, his voice barely above a whisper. "In the lobby."

"Wait there," she said quickly. "I'm coming."

He closed his eyes for a moment, the phone still pressed to his ear after the call ended. The air in the lobby felt heavier now, the smell of old paint clinging to the walls. He leaned against the cold glass of the front doors, staring out into the darkness.

***

When she approached him moments later, her footsteps echoed faintly on the marble floor. Her face was soft with concern now, the earlier brusqueness replaced by something gentler.

"Sorry to hear about your father," she began, her voice careful. "My mother told me. How are you holding up?"

He looked away, his eyes settling on the floor. "It's okay," he replied after a pause. "I have to be more responsible now."

Her gaze lingered on him, searching. "Life never stops," she said quietly. "But it teaches us, always."

He nodded absently, the words brushing against him without settling. "Funny, isn't it?" he said after a moment, a ghost of a smile playing on his lips. "People look at me like I'm a grown man, but I feel... I feel like a child playing dress-up."

She frowned slightly, tilting her head. "You need to step up," she said, her tone firmer now, though not unkind.

The smile widened, stretched tight across his face. It felt like a mask, and he wore it well. "Yes, yes," he said, a faint edge creeping into his voice. "Get a job. Then die, just like my father."

Ridhi blinked, startled, but said nothing.

He looked at her, and for a moment, the mask cracked. "Take care of yourself," she said softly, her voice almost pleading. "If you ever need anything, you know you can call me."

He gave a sharp laugh, bitter and hollow. "I don't think I'll give you that favour. Goodbye."

He turned to leave but hesitated. "By the way," he added, his voice lighter, almost casual. "Your father... he's still at the same school, right?"

She frowned. "Yes. Why?"

"Just... curious." He didn't wait for her response. Instead, he walked away, the air between them thick with unfinished thoughts.

***

In Late afternoon of  the following day , the school loomed ahead like a brooding sentinel, its red-brick facade darkened by the weight of time and rusted iron gates that creaked under the burden of forgotten stories. Ramesh stood before it, his silhouette framed against the pale evening sky, where streaks of purple bled into the descending gloom. His hands were buried deep in his back pockets, fingers clenched into fists against the cool fabric, each deliberate step toward the building heavy with purpose.

The corridors stretched like veins, winding endlessly under a patchwork of flickering fluorescent lights. The air was dense, laden with the faint tang of chalk dust mingled with the earthy scent of old wood polish. Bulletin boards lined the walls, cluttered with yellowing announcements—a chaotic timeline of achievements and reminders now irrelevant to the present. Ramesh's footsteps echoed in the silence, a rhythm both haunting and resolute, as if each step carried the weight of years lost and decisions made.

Stopping before the principal's office, he glanced at the nameplate. The brass letters gleamed dully, an unassuming marker for the man who had loomed so large in his life. He lingered for a moment, his lips curling into a faint, sardonic smile before the peon's sharp voice broke the silence.

"Yes?" The man's gaze flicked up from his newspaper, narrowing as it settled on Ramesh.

"I need to meet the principal," Ramesh said, his voice measured, calm.

"For what?"

Ramesh's smile deepened, humourless, almost bitter. "He'll want to see me. I proposed to his daughter once."

The peon's eyes widened, caught between disbelief and the uncomfortable urge to laugh. "Your name?"

"Ramesh."

There was a pause, a hesitation that seemed to stretch the air taut. Finally, the peon disappeared behind the office door, his retreating steps quick and uncertain.

When the door reopened, Ramesh was ushered inside. The principal's office stood in stark contrast to the dim corridors—a room of sterile order, its walls adorned with certificates of merit and framed photographs of beaming students. Behind the meticulously arranged desk sat Ridhi's father, his imposing figure softened only slightly by the creases of age. The crisp lines of his shirt and the gleaming pen in his pocket spoke of discipline, a life governed by unflinching rules.

"Ramesh." The principal's voice carried the same clipped authority that had commanded classrooms. "It's been a long time. Sit, sit. How are you? I heard about your father. Tragic." His words, though polite, were distant, perfunctory. "What brings you here?"

Ramesh lowered himself into the chair, but his posture remained tense, leaning forward as if preparing for battle. His eyes met the older man's without wavering.

"Sir," he began, his tone quiet but unyielding, "I love your daughter. I want to marry her."

The room seemed to grow colder. The principal's expression froze, his façade of politeness splintering. "What?" His voice cut through the air, sharp, disbelieving. "When? Why hasn't she said anything to me?"

"She loves me too," Ramesh continued evenly, each word a calculated strike. "In fact, she proposed. We're getting married tomorrow. Or the day after." He leaned closer. "I thought you should know."

The chair scraped loudly against the floor as the principal shot to his feet. "Stand up," he barked, his voice trembling with fury. "I said, *stand up!*"

Ramesh rose slowly, his movements deliberate, almost languid. The storm brewing in the room seemed to center around him, his expression calm, unreadable.

"You're insane," the principal hissed, his composure crumbling. "An idiot. You think you can waltz in here and—"

But the words never finished. Ramesh's hand moved with startling speed, seizing the principal's arm as it reached for the phone. The flash of steel was sudden, almost surreal, as the blade plunged into the older man's chest. For a moment, time seemed to stutter, the principal's face frozen in wide-eyed shock before his body crumpled over the desk, lifeless.

Ramesh stood still, his breathing heavy, the knife gleaming in his hand. The room's silence was deafening, broken only by the faint hum of the air conditioner and the rhythmic drip of blood pooling onto the floor.

The door creaked open behind him. The peon stepped in, oblivious to the scene until his eyes fell on the slumped figure at the desk. He froze, his lips parting in a silent gasp. But Ramesh moved with eerie precision, closing the distance in an instant. The struggle was brief, mechanical. Moments later, the peon lay motionless, his blood mingling with the principal's, dark rivulets seeping into the cracks of the wooden floor.

***

The metallic tang of blood lingered in the still air, clinging to Ramesh's clothes and skin as he stepped over the lifeless bodies sprawled across the polished wood floor. The principal's hand, stiff and pale, hung off the edge of the desk, fingers curling into the void like a futile grasp for salvation. The peon lay crumpled in a heap near the door, his face frozen in an expression of quiet disbelief. Ramesh paused at the threshold of the principal's office, his chest rising and falling in measured rhythm, though his breath felt distant, mechanical, as though it belonged to someone else entirely.

With a sharp click, he locked the door behind him and turned, his footsteps reverberating through the labyrinthine corridors of the school. The sound echoed, hollow and steady, the cadence of a man unburdened by haste. The fluorescent lights flickered erratically, casting long shadows that seemed to dance along the walls. The air felt heavy, pressing against him with the weight of all that had transpired, yet Ramesh moved forward with the tranquility of a man who had already crossed the precipice of consequence.

The open sky greeted him at the school gates, streaked with deep hues of orange and purple, the fading remnants of daylight folding into the embrace of evening . A breeze stirred the air, carrying with it the faint scent of rain mingled with the city's grime. Ramesh slipped into his car, his hands steady as they gripped the steering wheel. The ignition sputtered to life, and the radio flickered on, flooding the car with an upbeat tune. A jangly guitar riff played over cheerful lyrics, a cruel contrast to the storm brewing inside him.

**The road stretched ahead,** an endless ribbon of asphalt glowing faintly under the pale . The steady hum of the engine filled the car, a sound both monotonous and strangely comforting. It provided a backdrop to Ramesh's restless thoughts—fragments of memories and emotions colliding like shards of glass.

Ridhi's face loomed large in his mind, her eyes wide with unspoken words. He could still hear her voice, trembling with a fragile kind of hope as she spoke of dreams they'd once imagined sharing. But those dreams had crumbled into dust, their weight pressing heavily on his chest. He shook his head, trying to dislodge the image, but it clung to him like a stubborn shadow.

Then came the principal's sneer, the sharpness of his contempt slicing through the air like a blade. The memory burned, leaving behind an ache that refused to fade. And finally, the flash of steel—bright and fleeting—plunging into flesh that yielded with chilling ease. The resistance had been brief, as though even the body understood the futility of fighting against the inevitable.

A jagged laugh escaped Ramesh's lips, startling even him. It was raw and unhinged, a sound that didn't seem to belong to him. Glancing at the rearview mirror, he caught sight of his own reflection. His face was calm, almost serene, but his eyes were wild—twin abysses that seemed to swallow the faint light around them.

As the car neared his house, the familiar landmarks blurred together, their familiarity offering no solace. He parked and climbed the stairs, each step echoing dully in the silence of the evening. When he pushed the door open, the quiet inside was overwhelming, pressing against him like a physical weight. The small room seemed to shrink around him, its walls narrowing with every breath he took.

Ramesh closed the door behind him and leaned against it, his chest rising and falling as though he had run a marathon. For a brief moment, he stood still, the only sound in the room the faint hum of electricity. Then, as though propelled by an unseen force, he began to move.

The first chair shattered against the wall with an explosion of sound, the wood splintering into jagged pieces. It felt good. Liberating. The act of destruction filled the  space inside him, each crash and crack silencing the chaos in his mind, if only for a moment. He grabbed a bookshelf next, tipping it forward. Its contents—books, knickknacks, and dust-covered memories— spilled to the floor in a cacophony of noise.

The drawers of the kitchen cabinets were next. He yanked them open, their contents scattering across the tile in a chaotic symphony of clattering silverware and broken glass. The destruction was intoxicating, each ruined object stripping away the layers of control he had clung to for so long.

Then he saw it: his mother's photograph. The frame rested on a side table, untouched amidst the chaos. He hesitated for a moment, his breath catching in his throat. The picture was an anchor, tethering him to a version of himself he no longer recognized. With trembling hands, he picked it up. Her face— gentle, familiar, and impossibly distant—looked back at him through the cracked glass.

A single tear traced a path down his cheek, and for a moment, he felt the weight of his grief pressing down on him. "I'm sorry," he whispered, his voice cracking under the strain of the admission. He placed the photograph back on the table, careful not to disturb the shards of glass scattered around it. Then he turned away, his expression hardening once more.

In the kitchen, the stove stood silent and unassuming, a mundane fixture in a room now transformed into a battlefield. Ramesh crouched before it, his fingers brushing the knobs as though performing a sacred ritual. He turned one, and a spark ignited. The blue-orange flame sprang to life, its flickering light casting shadows across his face. He stared into it. The heat warmed his skin, but the fire itself felt cold—indifferent to the destruction it promised.

Outside, the distant sound of sirens and shrieks of vendors began to rise, faint at first but growing louder with each passing second. Ramesh didn't move. He stayed rooted to the spot, his eyes fixed on the flames. The acrid smell of smoke filled the room, curling upward in delicate spirals that seemed to mock the chaos surrounding him.

The sirens became a wail, piercing through the stillness of the evening . He heard hurried footsteps in the hallway, voices shouting in alarm. The door to his house burst open with a deafening crash, and a group of officers stormed inside. The sight that greeted them was surreal—a room in shambles, smoke curling lazily toward the ceiling, and Ramesh, kneeling before the stove, his back to them.

"Ramesh!" one of the officers called out, his voice sharp and commanding. "Step away from the fire."

But Ramesh didn't respond. He stayed where he was, his silhouette bathed in the flickering light of the flames. The heat was intense now, searing his skin and filling his lungs with the bitter taste of smoke.

The officer stepped closer, his hand hovering over the weapon at his side. "Ramesh," he said again, his tone softer this time, almost pleading. "Please. We can talk."

Finally, Ramesh moved. He tilted his head slightly, as though considering the words. A faint smile flickered across his lips—small, enigmatic, and utterly unreadable. Slowly, he turned to face them. His eyes, reflecting the wild dance of the dim flames. He opened a packet that he had taken from Tony , sniffed it hard . One of the officers lunged forward, grabbing Ramesh's arm and pulling him away from the stove. The fire hissed and roared in protest, but its heat began to fade as another officer turned off the gas. Ramesh didn't resist. His body felt light , as though the energy that had driven him moments ago had drained away completely.

They led him out of the house , the cool evening air a stark contrast to the oppressive heat inside. He looked up at the sky, their light distant and indifferent, and for a moment, he felt like he is in shoot of a hollywood movie .

As they loaded him into the back of the police car, he glanced back at the building. Smoke still poured from the windows, but the flames were gone . Ramesh leaned his head against the cool glass of the car window, his eyes closing as exhaustion overtook him .

He nestled down on the back seat of police car and started watching a sitcom on his smart phone .

www.ingramcontent.com/pod-product-compliance
Lightning Source LLC
Chambersburg PA
CBHW020346180726
47991CB00021B/2887